MW00475065

SAI BABA

The Divine Fakir

An imprint of Om Books International

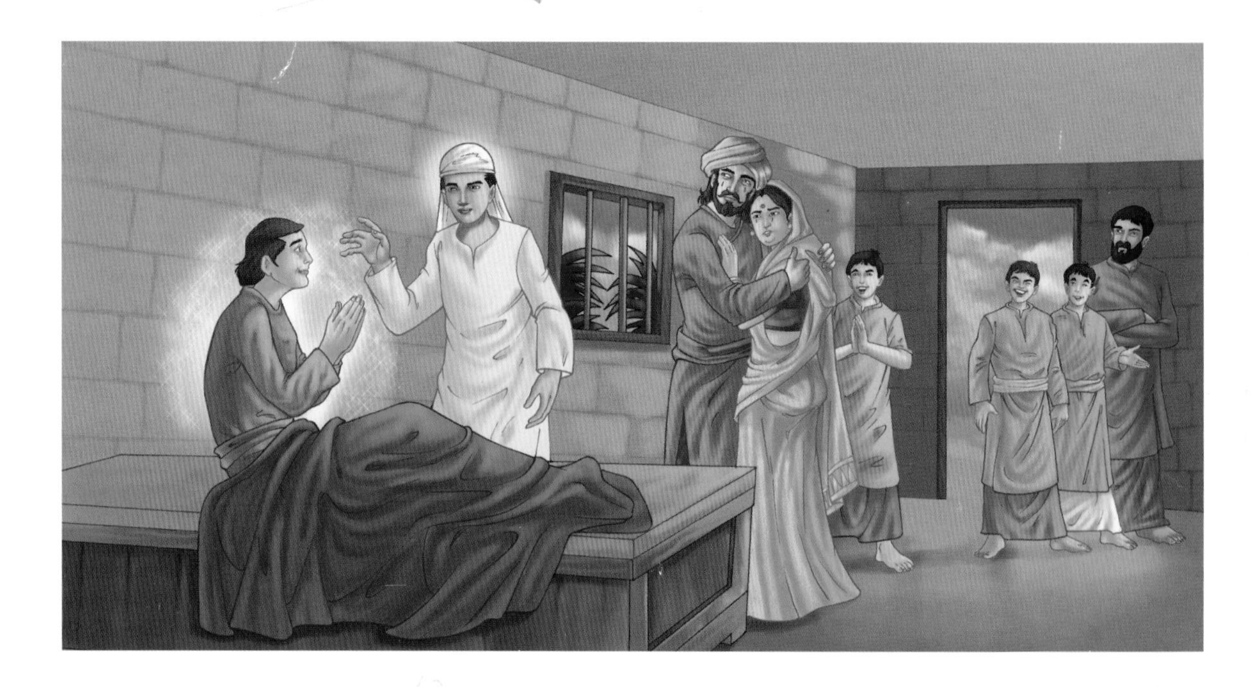

First Reprint 2012

Published by

An imprint of Om Books International

Corporate & Editorial Office
A 12, Sector 64, Noida 201 301
Uttar Pradesh, India
Phone: +91 120 477 4100
Email: editorial@ombooks.com
Website: www.ombooksinternational.com

Sales Office
4379/4B, Prakash House, Ansari Road
Darya Ganj, New Delhi 110 002, India
Phone: +91 11 2326 3363, 2326 5303
Fax: +91 11 2327 8091
Email: sales@ombooks.com
Website: www.ombooks.com

Copyright © Om Books International 2009

ALL RIGHTS RESERVED. No part of this book may be reproduced or transmitted in any form by any means, electronic or mechanical, including photocopying and recording, or by any information storage and retrieval system, except as may be expressly permitted in writing by the publisher.

ISBN : 978-81-87108-42-9

Printed in India

10 9 8 7 6 5 4 3 2

Contents

This book is only a reproduction of the various divine works on Baba's life and teachings. Since there is no clear indication on Baba's birth, an attempt has been made to put together stories from the Sai Sacharita, Sai Leela and other such resources.

Sai's Divine Birth

Some believe that in the year 1835, Baba was born to a brahmin couple called Gangabhavaidya and Vedagiri Amma, in Pathri village, in the Indian state of Maharashtra. Unfortunately, Baba lost his parents at a very young age, and was handed over by a few relatives to a Fakir. The Fakir looked after him

till the year 1839 and then died. His wife handed over the child to a Guru (teacher) named Venkusa. Baba stayed in Guru Venkusa's ashram (school) for twelve years.

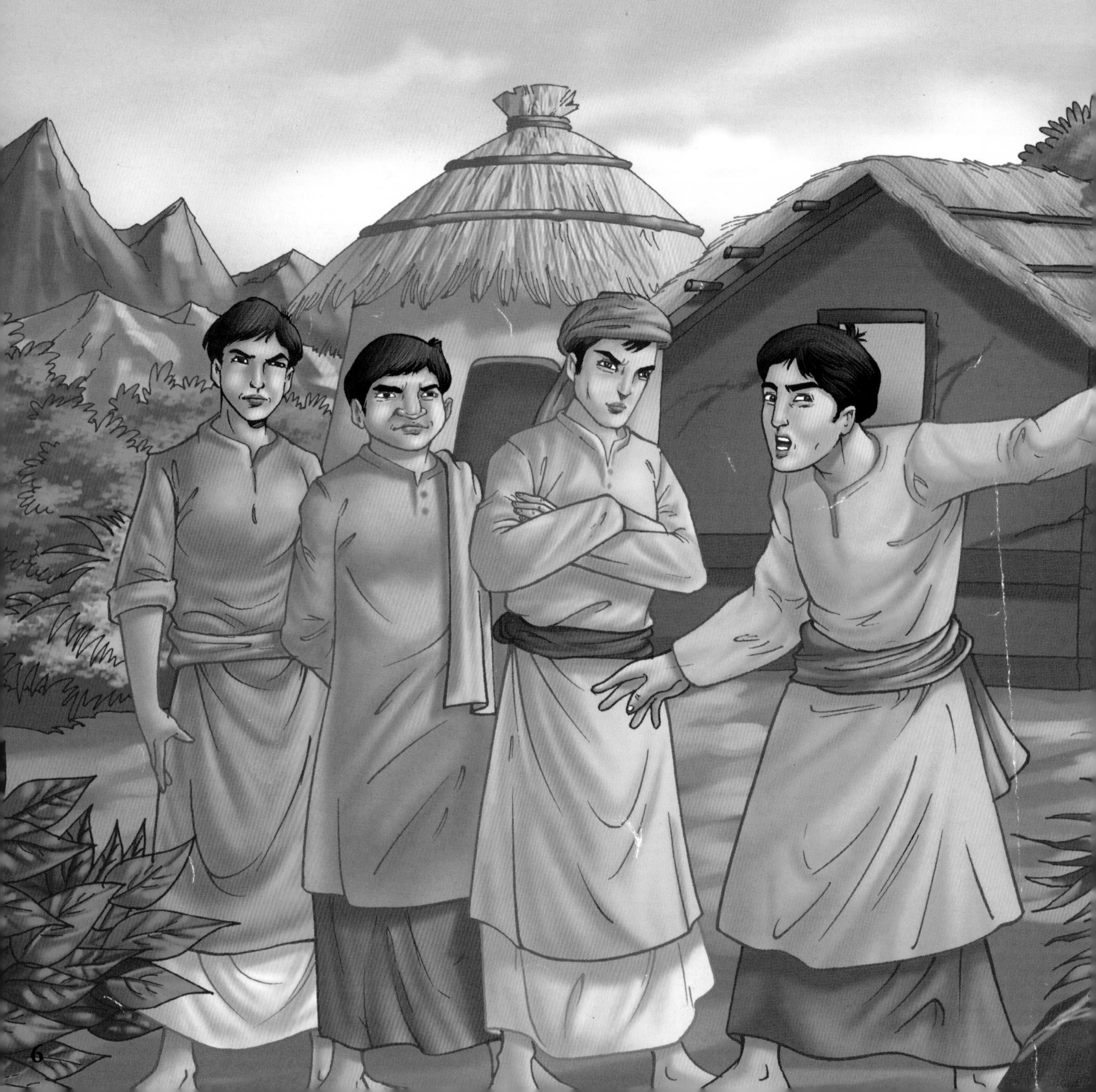

Guru Venkusa knew that Baba was no ordinary boy and looked after him with a lot of devotion and care. This made the other boys in the ashram jealous of Baba. "Why is Baba so special?" asked one of the students in Guru

Venkusa's ashram. "He always gets the attention of our teacher," said the other. "It's time we teach him a lesson," declared another boy.

Finally, one of the boys threw a brick at Baba's head while he was walking. Baba was

injured, but the boy who tried to kill him died mysteriously. Baba took pity on the dead boy and performed the miracle of bringing him back to life. This is believed to be the first of Baba's miracles.

Another story of his divine birth says that Sai Baba was born to a boatman. The story goes that Baba's father – Bavaidya – was very poor. One day, while he was away fishing, his wife – Devagiri Amma – was alone at home. They had no children.

Lord Shiva, disguised as an old man, came to their house asking for food and shelter. Devagiri Amma served him with great devotion and respect. "You will be blessed with three children – two sons and a daughter. One of your sons will be an incarnation of mine," said Lord Shiva, pleased with Amma's devotion.

Devagiri Amma gave birth to three children, but had to abandon one of her sons under a peepal tree, as they had to leave the village because of poverty. Being poor, she could not take all her children with her, and so abandoned one of them.

A muslim couple who was passing by the forest, saw the baby covered with peepal leaves. "What a divine face," exclaimed the wife. "Let us adopt him as God's blessing," said the husband and they took the baby home. A few years later,

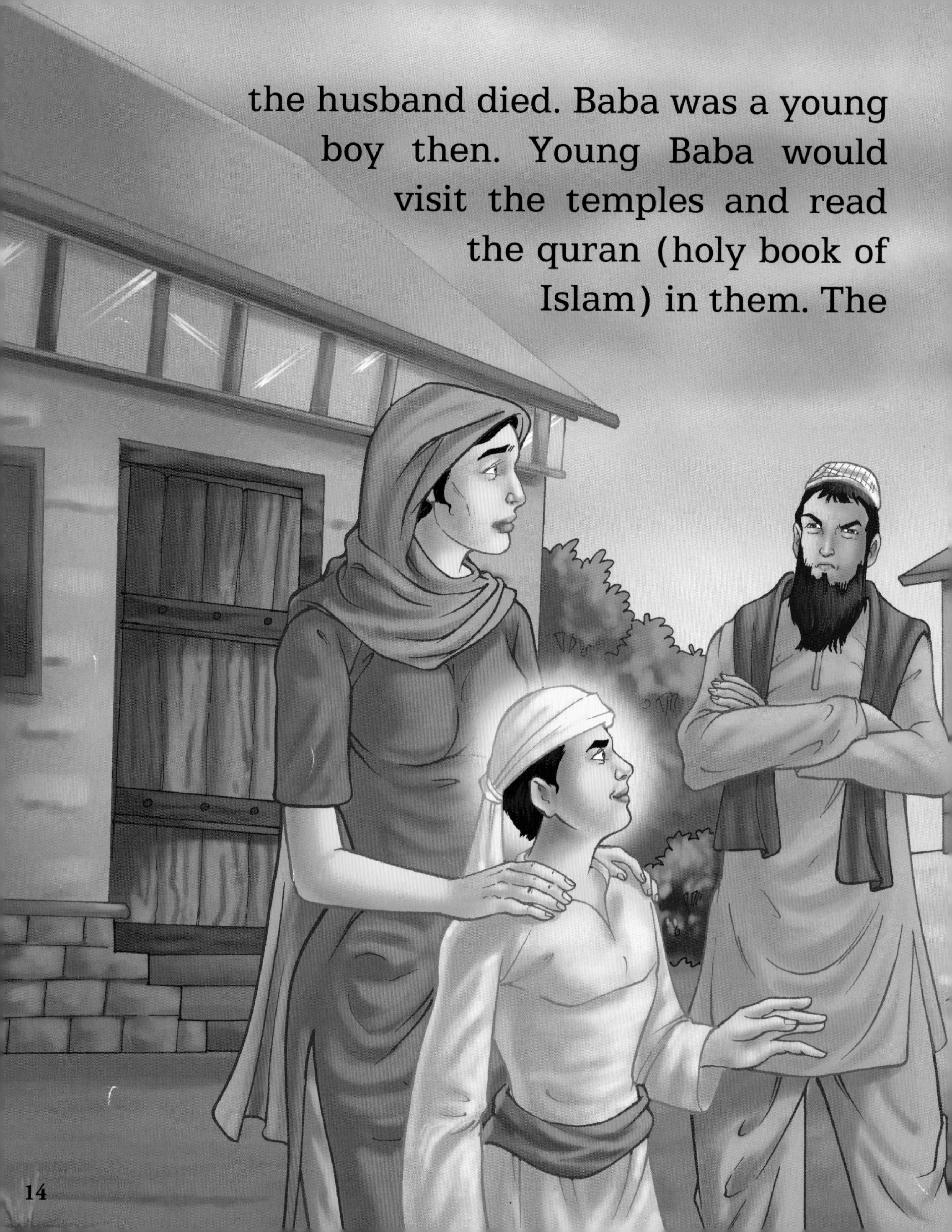

the husband died. Baba was a young boy then. Young Baba would visit the temples and read the quran (holy book of Islam) in them. The villagers did not like this and complained to his mother. Unable to change Baba's behaviour, his mother left him in the care of Guru Venkusa, in his ashram.

Sai Baba and the Oil Merchants

It was Baba's daily ritual to light lamps in the mosque every evening. He would go to the oil merchants in Shirdi and beg for oil. "Please give me some oil," Baba would request one of the merchants. However, the merchants were not too happy

giving him oil every day. "Oil does not come for free. How can he beg for oil every day?" they asked one another.

"Let us refuse to give him oil when he comes today," said one of the merchants. That day, all of them refused Baba. "Baba, there is no oil to spare. Please go away," they said.

Baba returned to the mosque. The merchants followed him. "Let's see what he does today," they said to each other. Baba picked up a can of water and poured it into the lamps. "Did I not tell you all that he is mad?" exclaimed one of the merchants.

Before the others could answer, they saw Baba lighting the lamps. The lamps burned brightly, silencing everyone who was there.

The merchants fell at Baba's feet begging for forgiveness. "Baba, we have been mean to you. Please forgive us," they cried.

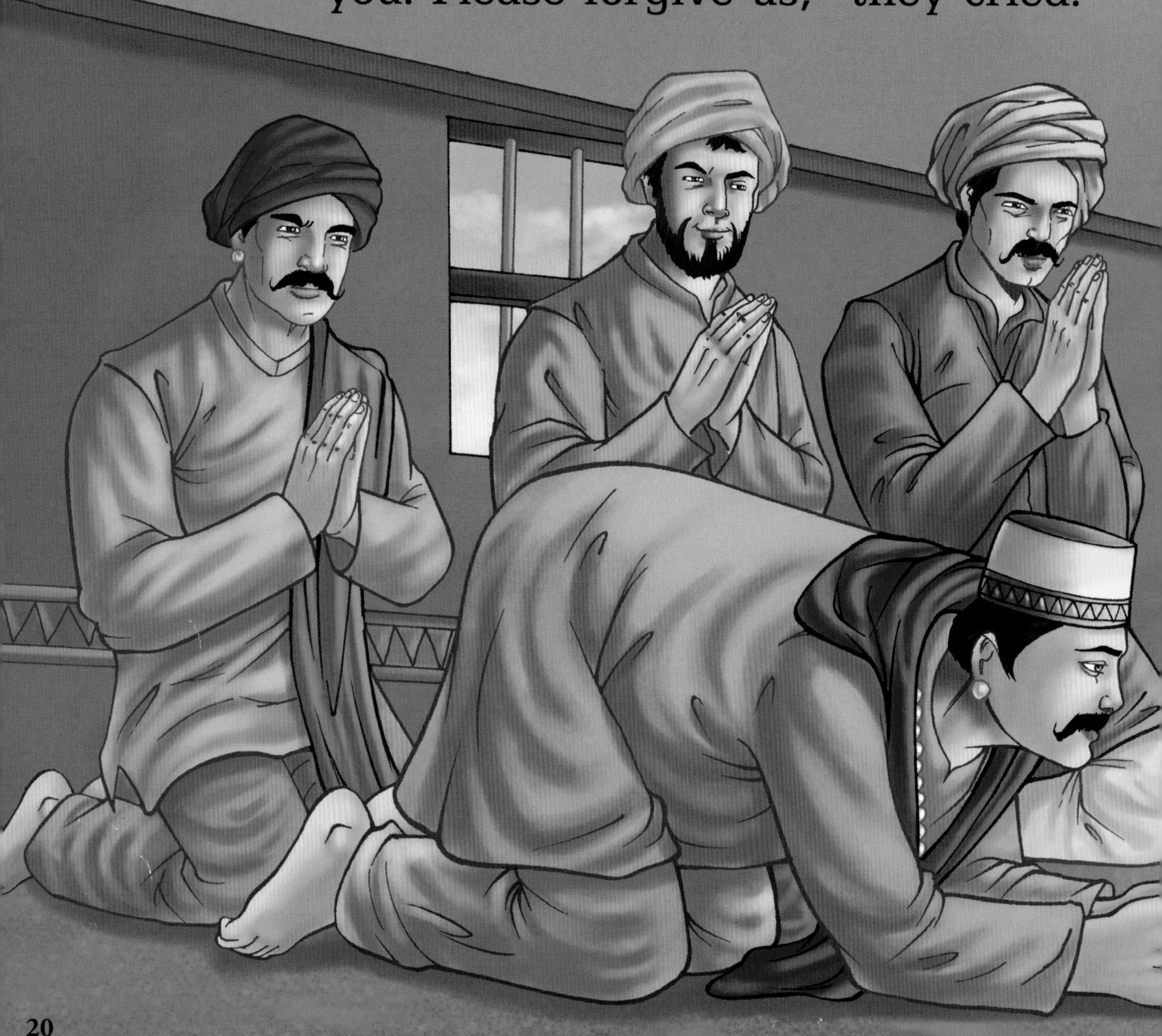

"Never tell a lie! You need not have told me that you had no oil to spare, when you did have it. Since you have repented on your act, God has already forgiven you," said Baba asking them to rise. Such was Baba's forgiving nature!

Sai Baba Comes to Shirdi

It is believed that Sai Baba lived under a tree for many years as a young boy. He then disappeared and after a few years returned to Shirdi.

The story goes like this...

Chand Patil, an officer in the remote village of Dhoopkede (a village in Aurangabad, Maharashtra) was on his way to a wedding.

He had lost his horse in the forest and was looking for it. "Where could it have gone?" wondered Chand, when he heard a voice. "Why don't you rest for a while? You look very tired." Chand turned around to see a young

man clad in white clothes, like a saint, sitting on a rock.

The young man was Baba. "What brings you to this dense forest, Chand bhai?" asked Baba. Chand was wonderstruck. 'How could

he have known my name?' he thought to himself. "I have lost my horse," he replied.

"Look behind those trees Chand, and you will find what you are looking for," said Baba. Chand found his horse exactly where Baba had guided him. He took his horse and knew

at once, that Baba was no ordinary man. He returned to Baba and asked him who he was and where he was headed.

"People call me Sai Baba. I have no destination," he replied. "In that case, why don't you come with me Baba. My wife's

nephew is getting married in Shirdi, and we would be honoured to have you as our guest," requested Chand. Baba accepted his invitation and accompanied him to Shirdi. After the wedding, Baba stayed on at Shirdi.

One day, Baba went to Khandoba's temple, thinking that he would make it his home. But he was met at the gate by the temple priest, Mhalsapathy. "If you are looking for the mosque, it is right round that corner," said Mhalsapathy. Baba merely smiled and walked away.

Baba found his home in the mosque nearby, where he lived from that day on.

But he had left a deep impression on Mhalsapathy, who felt that the man he had turned away was no ordinary one. Years later, he became one of Baba's greatest devotees. It is also believed that Baba told him that he was born to a brahmin couple in Pathri village.

Baba Saves Helpless Farmers

Harvesting in Shirdi was always a delightful activity. The farmers looked after their corn fields with great care throughout the year for a good harvest at the end of it.

But one summer, during the harvesting season, it was unusually hot. A number of people had died because of the heat.

Baba called Kondaji Sutar and said, "Your field is on fire. Go immediately!" Kondaji was very frightened and ran to his field. However, after looking around the field for quite some time, Kondaji could not find any fire. He returned to Baba. "Baba, everything is fine with my field. There is no sign of any fire," he said. "Look carefully! Go back and check," insisted Baba.

Kondaji obeyed Baba's orders and went back to his field. This time, he saw that one of the sheaves of corn had indeed caught fire. With a strong wind blowing, that fire started spreading swiftly. "Baba! Save us! Save us Baba!" screamed the helpless farmers.

Baba arrived at the scene and saw the plight of the farmers. "Baba, save us before we and our families are ruined," they cried. Baba poured some water into his palm and sprinkled it over a few sheaves. Within seconds, the fire was doused. The farmers were beyond themselves with joy. Baba had saved their harvest!

Baba Saves His Devotee

Damodar Savalram Rasne, also known as Damu Anna was an ardent devotee of Baba, and lived in Mumbai. Damu Anna's friend had written to him seeking his partnership for starting a business in cotton.

Damu Anna never undertook anything without Baba's consent. So he decided to write a letter to Shama, Baba's devotee and close aide. "Please consult Baba about my starting a business in cotton, and advise," requested Damu Anna.

When Shama received the letter, he read it out to Baba. "Tell him not to become greedy. God has given him a lot. Tell Damu to be contented with what he has and not to waste his time in pursuing worldly pleasures," advised Baba. Shama wrote Baba's advice in a letter and posted it to Damu Anna.

Damu Anna trusted Baba's advice so much that he wrote to his friend refusing to take up the partnership.

That year, the cotton crop failed miserably. Everyone who had put in money into the cotton trade incurred huge losses. Damu Anna was saved by Baba's advice.

A few years later, Damu Anna wanted to trade in paddy. So he again consulted Baba on starting his business. Strangely, Baba accepted the idea this time. "If you purchase

at 7 seers a rupee, remember to sell it at 9 seers a rupee," said Baba. It was unimaginable to think of selling at a lower price than what it was bought at. But Damu Anna's devotion made him obey Baba's orders.

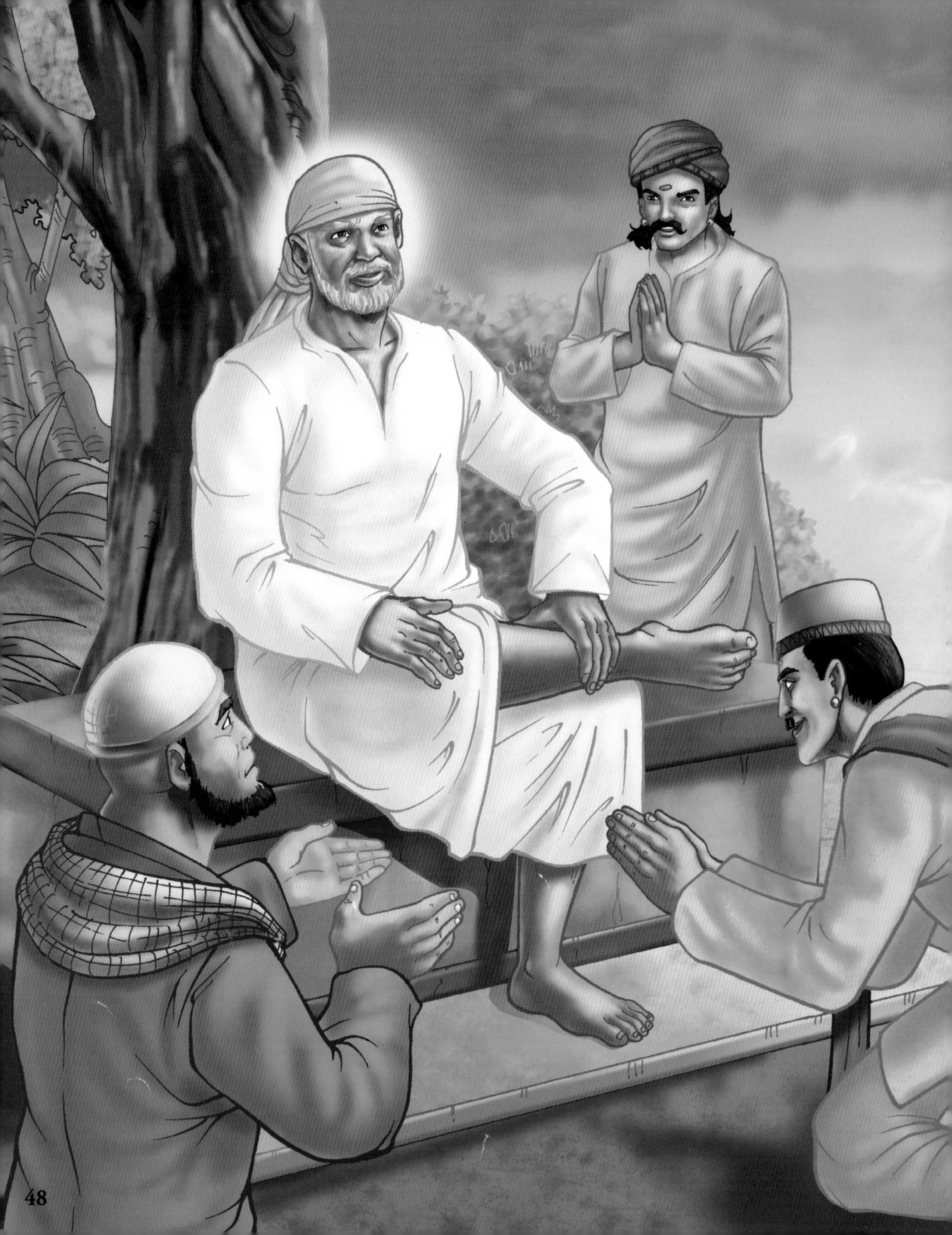

That year, the price of paddy was lower than ever before. Every merchant who hoarded paddy in his godown incurred huge losses. Damu Anna was saved, once again, by Baba's sound advice.

But Damu Anna was worried. He thought of the time ahead when Baba would not be there in this Earthly world. Baba read his thoughts. "I will always be there for my devotees in one form or the other. I will respond to their needs at all times, if I am remembered," said Baba reassuring Damu Anna.

Baba's Miraculous Powers

Shirdi was overflowing with devotees as usual. One day, two men arrived at Shirdi from Goa. They walked to Dwarkamai, where Baba lived.

The men sat amongst the hundreds of devotees waiting to see Baba. Baba never disappointed his devotees. He patiently walked across the rows of devotees giving them the famous Udi (also known as Vibhuti or sacred ash).

When Baba saw the two men, he asked one for fifteen rupees. "Baba, please accept thirty-

five rupees," replied the man humbly putting forward the money. "I neither ask for more nor for what I am not destined," said Baba and asked again for fifteen rupees. The man gave fifteen rupees and prayed to Baba with folded hands. Then Baba suddenly started telling stories in his strange manner.

"I was eager to get my first job. I prayed to Lord Dattatreya that I would offer my first month's salary to him, if I got the job. Dattatreya was indeed kind and blessed me with my first job. I joined the job and got fifteen rupees as my first month's salary. But, I forgot my vow to Dattatreya. I lived my life without fulfilling my vow," said Baba and took a deep breath.

Shama, Baba's devotee and close aide looked at Baba puzzled. Then Shama turned to the man who had given Baba the money. He was crying bitterly. "Why are you weeping?" asked

Shama. “Baba rids anyone who comes to Shirdi of suffering. So, do not weep as you will soon find a solution to your suffering,” said Shama. “I have already been rid of my suffering,” said

the man. “The story that Baba narrated is mine. I had prayed to Dattatreya for my job and forgot to fulfill the promise I made about giving him my first salary,” said the man.

"Today Baba has taken the money from me and rid me of the debt I owed," added the man.

When the man had finished speaking, Baba began another story. "It was midnight and I was in deep sleep. Unknown to me, someone made a big hole in the wall and stole thirty thousand rupees. When I saw the hole in the morning, I was shocked. I was so sad that I could not eat or sleep for days together. Then a friend met me and advised me to pray to a saint. He told me that the saint would help me get back my money if I stopped eating

my favourite food item till I got back the money. I did what the friend told me and got back my money. Then I boarded a steamer, and was told that there was no room for me. But with the help of a servant serving on the steamer, I got some place for myself. Travelling by train after the steamer, I came to Shirdi," said Baba.

Hearing this, the second man started weeping. Wiping his tears after a few minutes, he said, "Baba has narrated my story this time. I had a cook who served me very well for many years. But greed got to him and he stole thirty thousand rupees from my house

while my family and I were sleeping. I was so distressed that I stopped eating for several days. My friend advised me to pray to Sai Baba and give up eating my favourite food till I got back my money. I did as my friend told me and got back my money," said the man.

Such was the miraculous power that Baba had. He knew the past, present and future of every one who came to visit him and never let down any of his devotees.

After both the men had spoken, Baba asked Shama to take them for their meals. Baba's concern for his devotees was admirable.

The Old Lady's Offering

There lived an old lady in Shirdi, who was an ardent devotee of Baba. She would bake two breads every day – one for herself and one for Baba. Then she would walk to the mosque where Baba lived and give him the bread. This was a routine she followed every single day, be it sunshine or rain!

One day, the lady was on her way to the mosque with the breads, when she saw a dog limping towards her. The lady was overcome by a feeling of sadness for the condition the

dog was in. It was suffering from a wound and looked very hungry. The old lady took pity on the dog and gave it one of the breads.

While the dog sat down to eat the bread hungrily, the lady continued her journey to the mosque. But, she was in for another surprise. She saw a pig walking towards her. It looked as if it was about to faint any moment with hunger. As the lady saw the pig totter on the road, she took pity. "What is the use of food, if it is not offered to the hungry?" she thought and offered the second bread to the pig.

Then she walked towards the mosque to meet Baba. "Today, I have nothing to offer you, Baba," she said. "I set out with the two breads I bring every day, but was met by two animals on the way. I took pity on them and gave them both the breads," she said apologetically. But to her surprise, Baba smiled. "Mother, you have

offered me not one but TWO breads today. I got the offering you gave to the dog and the pig," said Baba.

"How did you know that I was met by a dog and a pig?" asked the lady with surprise.

"Because I was both of them," replied Baba. "He who feeds hungry and helpless animals, feeds me," said Baba. Such was Baba's compassion for animals!

Baba lives on in this Earthly world in his Samadhi at Shirdi. Thousands of pilgrims flock to Shirdi for Baba's blessings. It is believed that every devotee is rid of his suffering the moment he steps into Shirdi. Miracles are seen every day at this holy place, where Baba's legacy lives on.

TITLES IN THIS SERIES

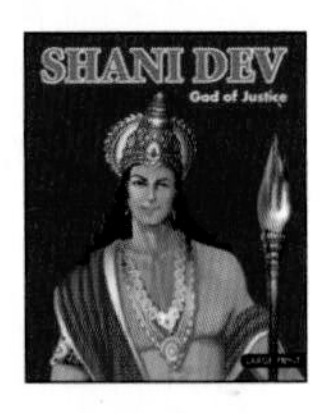